W9-AKU-435

The Snail and the Whale

by Julia Donaldson

pictures by Axel Scheffler

DIAL BOOKS FOR YOUNG READERS  NEW YORK

This is the tale of a tiny snail

And a great big, gray-blue humpback whale.

This is a rock as black as soot,

And this is a snail with an itchy foot.

The sea snail slithered all over the rock

And gazed at the sea and the ships in the dock.

And as she gazed, she sniffed and sighed.

"The sea is deep and the world is wide!

How I long to sail!"

Said the tiny snail.

These are the other snails in the flock,

Who all stuck tight to the smooth black rock

And said to the snail with the itchy foot,

"Be quiet! Don't wiggle! Sit still! Stay put!"

But the tiny sea snail sniffed and sighed,

Then cried, "I've got it! I'll hitch a ride!"

This is the trail

Of the tiny snail,

A silvery trail that looped and curled

And said, "Ride wanted around the world."

This is the whale who came one night

When the tide was high and the stars were bright.

A humpback whale, immensely long,

Who sang to the snail a wonderful song

Of shimmering ice and coral caves

And shooting stars and enormous waves.

And this is the tail

Of the humpback whale.

He held it out of the starlit sea

And said to the snail, "Come sail with me."

This is the sea,

So wild and free,

That carried the whale

And the snail on his tail

To towering icebergs and far-off lands,

With fiery mountains and golden sands.

These are the waves that arched and crashed,

That foamed and frolicked and sprayed

and SPLASHED

The tiny snail

On the tail of the whale.

These are the caves

Beneath the waves,

Where colorful fish with feathery fins

And sharks with hideous toothy grins

Swam past the whale

And the snail on his tail.

This is the sky,

So vast and high,

Sometimes sunny and blue and warm,

Sometimes filled with a thunderstorm,

With zigzag lightning

Flashing and frightening

The tiny snail

On the tail of the whale.

And she gazed at the sky, the sea, the land,

The waves and the caves and the golden sand.

She gazed and gazed, amazed by it all,

And she said to the whale, "I feel so small."

But then came the day

The whale lost his way . . .

These are the speedboats, running a race,

Zigging and zooming all over the place,

Upsetting the whale with their earsplitting roar,

Making him swim too close to the shore.

This is the tide, slipping away,

And this is the whale lying BEACHED in a bay.

"Quick! Off the sand! Back to sea!"
    cried the snail.
"I can't move on land! I'm too BIG!"
    moaned the whale.

The snail felt helpless and terribly small.
Then, "I've got it!" she cried,
    and started to crawl.

"I must not fail,"
Said the tiny snail.

This is the bell on the school in the bay,

Ringing the children in from their play.

This is the teacher, holding her chalk,

Telling the class, "Sit straight! Don't talk!"

This is the board, as black as soot,

And this is the snail with the itchy foot!

"A snail! A snail!"

The teacher turns pale.

"Look!" say the children.

    "It's leaving a trail."

This is the trail

Of the tiny snail,

A silvery trail saying, "SAVE THE WHALE."

These are the children, running from school,

Fetching the firemen, digging a pool,

Squirting and spraying to keep the whale cool.

This is the tide coming into the bay,

And these are the villagers shouting, "HOORAY!"

As the whale and the snail travel safely away . . .

Back to the dock

And the flock on the rock,

Who said, "How time's flown!"

And, "Haven't you grown!"

And the whale and the snail

Told their wonderful tale

Of shimmering ice and coral caves,

And shooting stars and enormous waves,

And of how the snail, so small and frail,

With her looping, curling, silvery trail,

Saved the life of the humpback whale.

Then the humpback whale

Held out his tail

And on crawled snail after snail after snail.

And they sang to the sea as they all set sail

On the tail of the gray-blue humpback whale.

For Malcolm—J.D.

First published in the United States 2004
by Dial Books for Young Readers
A division of Penguin Young Readers Group
345 Hudson Street • New York, New York 10014
Published in Great Britain 2003 by Macmillan Children's Books
Text copyright © 2003 by Julia Donaldson
Pictures copyright © 2003 by Axel Scheffler
All rights reserved
Printed in China

15 17 16

Library of Congress Cataloging-in-Publication Data
Donaldson, Julia.
The snail and the whale / by Julia Donaldson;
pictures by Axel Scheffler.
p.   cm.
Summary: Wanting to sail beyond its rock, a tiny snail hitches a ride
on a big humpback whale and then is able to help the whale
when it gets stuck in the sand.
ISBN 978-0-8037-2922-3
[1. Snails—Fiction. 2. Whales—Fiction. 3. Stories in rhyme.]
I. Scheffler, Axel. II. Title.
PZ8.3.D7235 Sn 2004   [E]—dc21   2003004133

*The art was created using pencil, ink,
watercolors, colored pencils, and crayons.*